CREATIVE
HAND
ART

b small publishing
www.bsmall.co.uk

Enjoying Hand Art

These activities encourage children to create beautiful and imaginative pictures of colourful animals, people, dinosaurs and creatures – or inventions from their own imagination! – using only the shapes that they can make with their hands, some coloured crayons and paint.

The step-by-step instructions guide children through a world of colours, shapes and messy fun. If you or your littles ones get fed up with one particular activity then just move on to the next one. If you really liked one then recreate it on a piece of scrap paper – or smart paper and frame it! Add your own designs and build on the suggestions in the book.

Children will enjoy creating their own pictures and will take great pride in what they have created. They will also be developing their hand-eye coordination and concentration skills, which will help later on with more formal learning, such as reading and writing.

To get started with creative hand art, you will need:
crayons or colouring pens or pencils, paint,
your hands or someone else's hands!

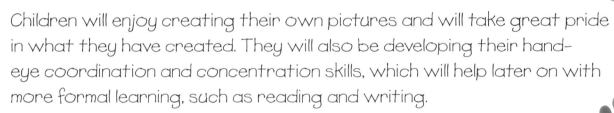

© 2012 Applebee Publishing Inc., Korea
This edition published by b small publishing ltd.
English translation © b small publishing, 2013

ISBN 978-1-908164-95-7

www.bsmall.co.uk

Activities: Sunny Kim   Illustrations: Kyunghee Yim

Printed in China by WKT Co. Ltd.

First published in the UK in 2013.

British Library Cataloguing-in-Publication Data.
A catalogue record for this book is available from the British Library.

Contents

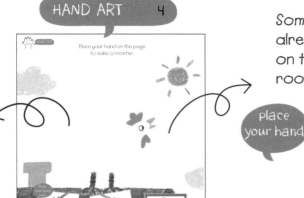

Some of the details are already waiting for you on the page such as this rooster's face and beak.

This area has been left blank for you to create your own picture.

place your hand

Follow the steps to create your picture. It's your creation so you can choose your own colours.

To make me you will need to get messy! Use your hand as a paintbrush. Be creative with colours.

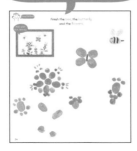

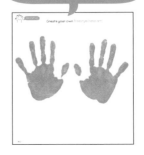

3

Place your hand on the page to make a rooster.

Place your hand here.

Draw round your hand.

Colour in the feathers.

Colour in the body.

4

 HAND ART

Place your hand on the page
to make a rabbit.

Place your hand here.

Draw round your hand.

+

Add the legs.

=

Colour in the body.

Place your hand on the page
to make a parrot.

Place your hand here.

Draw round your hand.   Colour in the feathers.   Colour in the body.

6

Place your hand on the page
to make a **swan**.

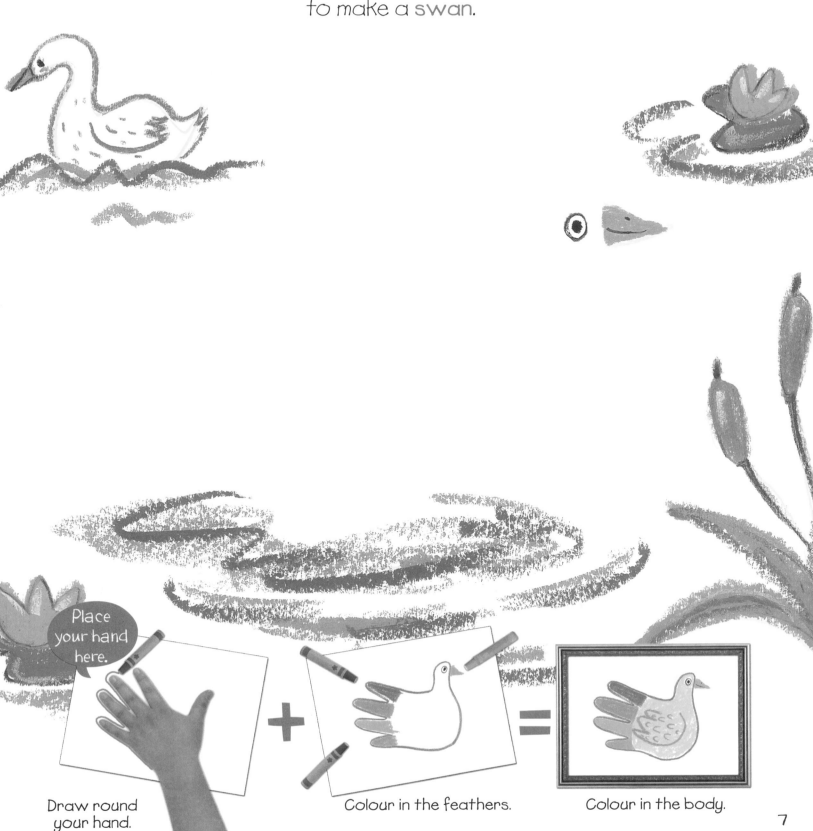

Place your hand here.

Draw round your hand.

Colour in the feathers.

Colour in the body.

7

Place your hand on the page to make a crane.

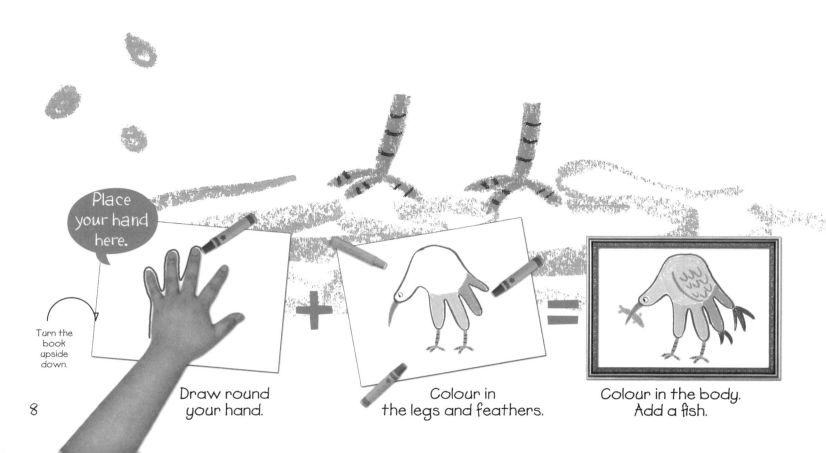

Place your hand here.

Turn the book upside down.

Draw round your hand.

Colour in the legs and feathers.

Colour in the body. Add a fish.

Place your hand on the page
to make a snail.

Place
your hand
here.

+

=

Draw round
your hand.

Add the rest of
the snail's body.

Colour in the shell.

HAND ART

Place your hand on the page
to complete the bear.

Place your hand here.

Draw round your hand.

Colour in the face.
Add eyes and a nose.

Colour in the ears.
Draw a mouth.

10

HAND ART

Place your hand on the page
to complete the monkey.

Place
your hand
here.

Draw round
your hand.

+

Complete the
rest of the monkey.

=

Colour in the body.

11

 HAND ART

Place your hand on the page
to make the **flying bird**.

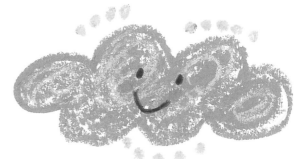

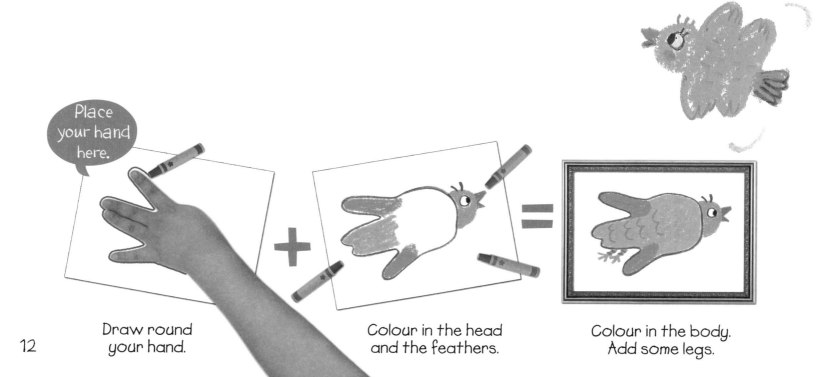

Place your hand here.

Draw round
your hand.

Colour in the head
and the feathers.

Colour in the body.
Add some legs.

12

Place your hand on the page
to make another flying bird.

Place
your hand
here.

+

=

Draw round
your hand.

Colour in the body.

Colour in the wings.
Add some legs.

13

Place your hand on the page to make a lion.

Place your hand here.

Turn the book upside down.

14

Draw round your hand.

+

Colour in the body
Draw the head.

=

Add feet and a tail.

Place your hand on the page
to make an **octopus**.

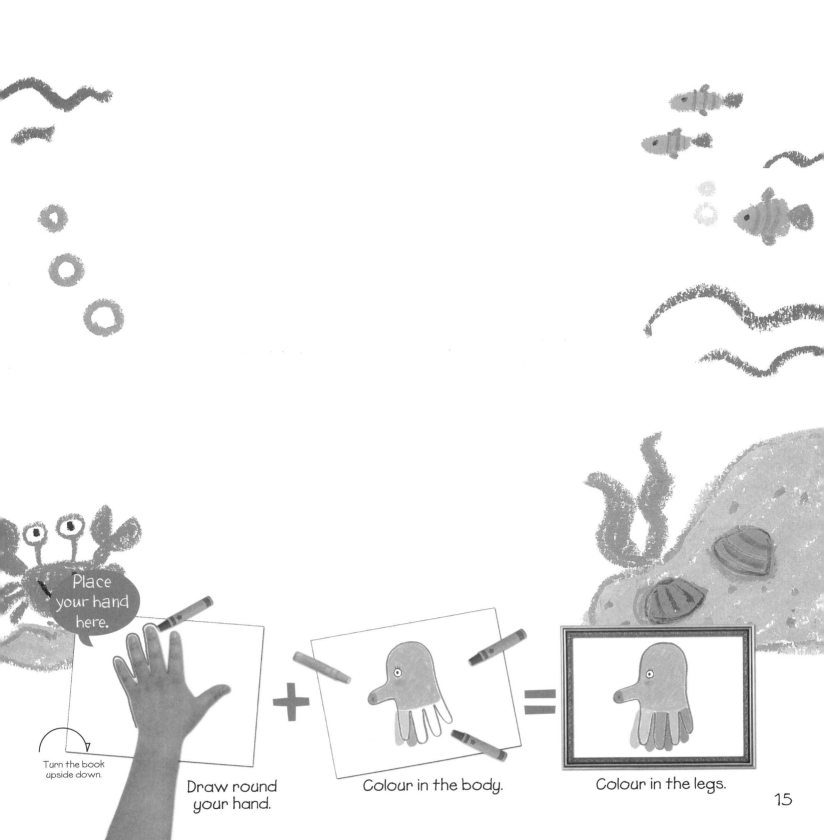

Place
your hand
here.

Turn the book
upside down.

Draw round
your hand.

+

Colour in the body.

=

Colour in the legs.

15

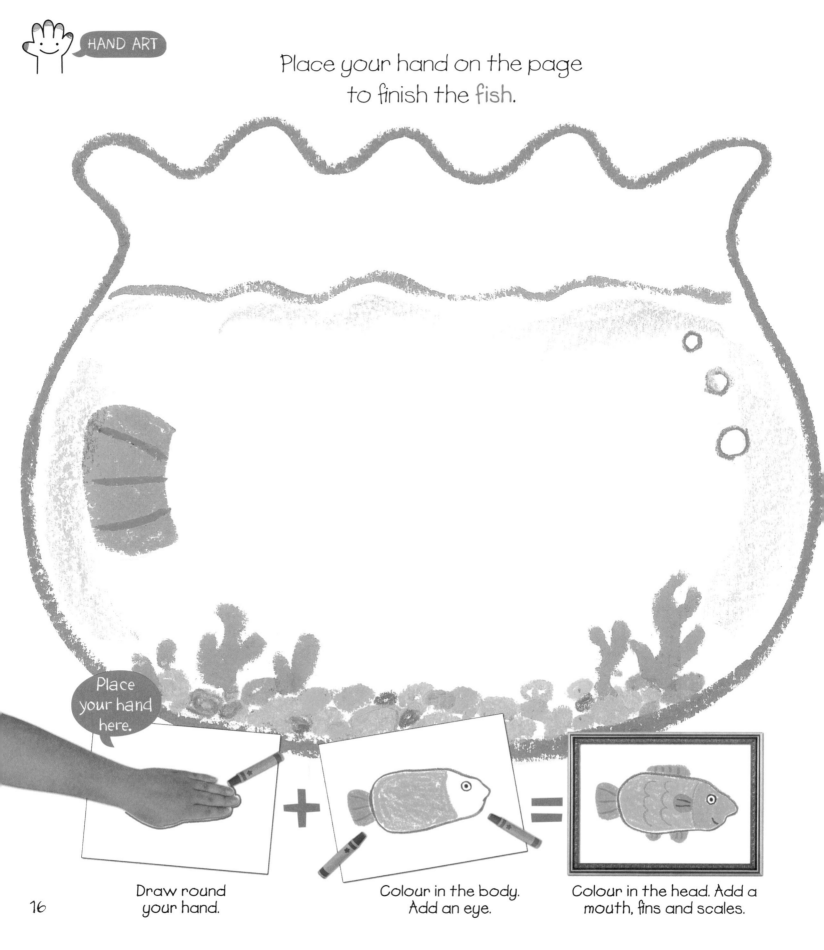

HAND ART

Place your hand on the page
to finish the fish.

Place your hand here.

Draw round
your hand.

+

Colour in the body.
Add an eye.

=

Colour in the head. Add a
mouth, fins and scales.

16

Place your hand on the page
to finish the **alligator**.

Place your hand here.

Draw round your hand.

Colour in the body. Draw in the nostrils.

Add scales and teeth.

17

Place your hand on the page
to finish the **dinosaur**.

Place
your hand
here.

Draw round
your hand.

Colour in the body.
Draw the face.

Add dermal plates
on the back.

Place your hand on the page
to finish the **butterfly**.

Place
your hand
here.

Draw round
your hand.

Add a second wing.
Start to colour it in.

Add patterns to the
body and wings.

19

 HAND ART

Place your hand on the page
to finish the **flower.**

Place
your hand
here.

Draw round
your hand.

Colour in the flower.

Add the stamens.

20

Place your hand on the page to complete the flower.

Place your hand here.

Draw round your hand.

Colour in the petals.

Add the stamens.

Place your hand on the page
to make a cabbage.

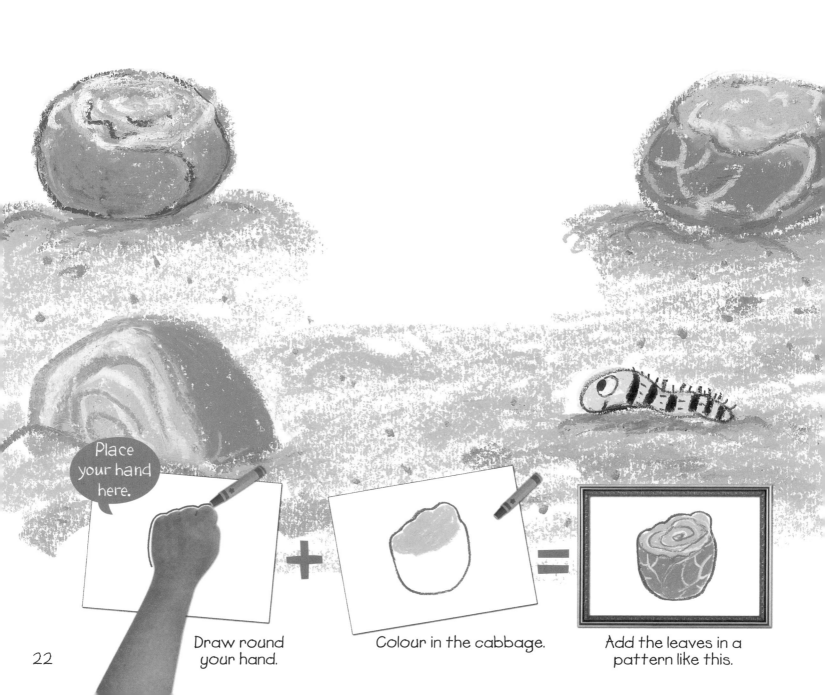

Place your hand here.

Draw round your hand.

Colour in the cabbage.

Add the leaves in a pattern like this.

22

Place your hand on the page
to finish the onion.

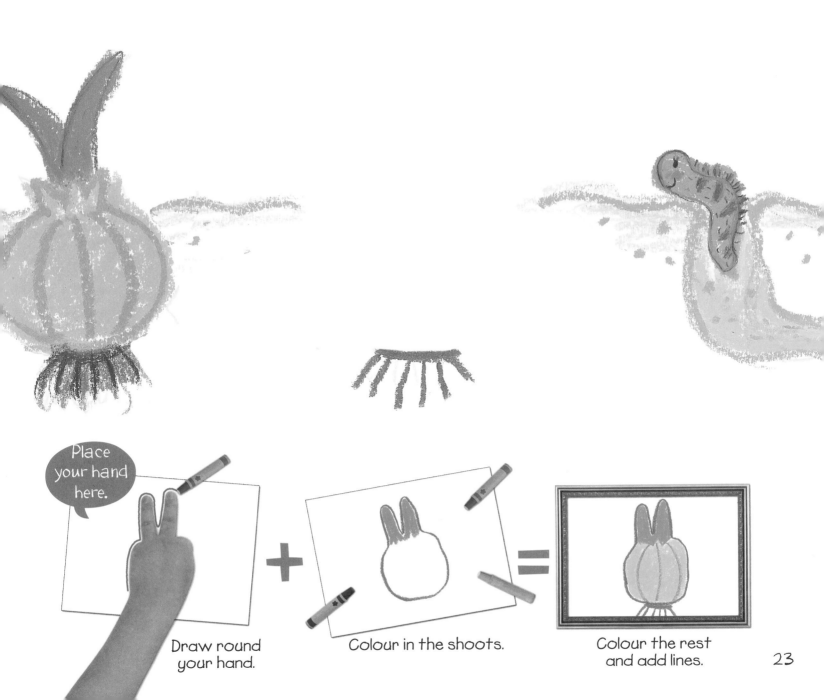

Place
your hand
here.

Draw round
your hand.

Colour in the shoots.

Colour the rest
and add lines.

23

Place your hand on the page to make
a Chinese cabbage.

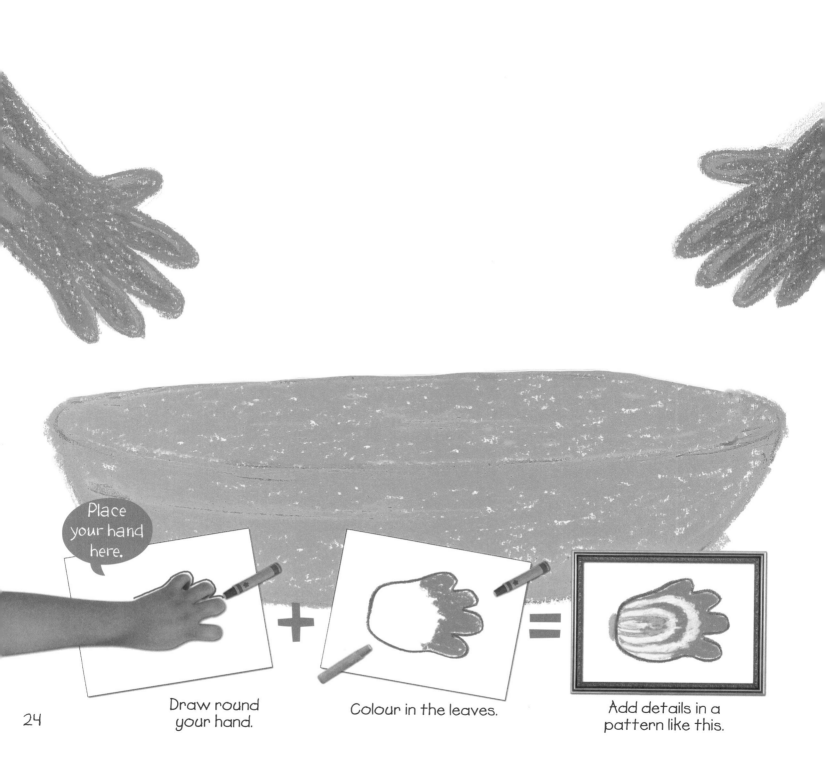

Place
your hand
here.

Draw round
your hand.

Colour in the leaves.

Add details in a
pattern like this.

 HAND ART

Place your hand on the page
to make a carrot.

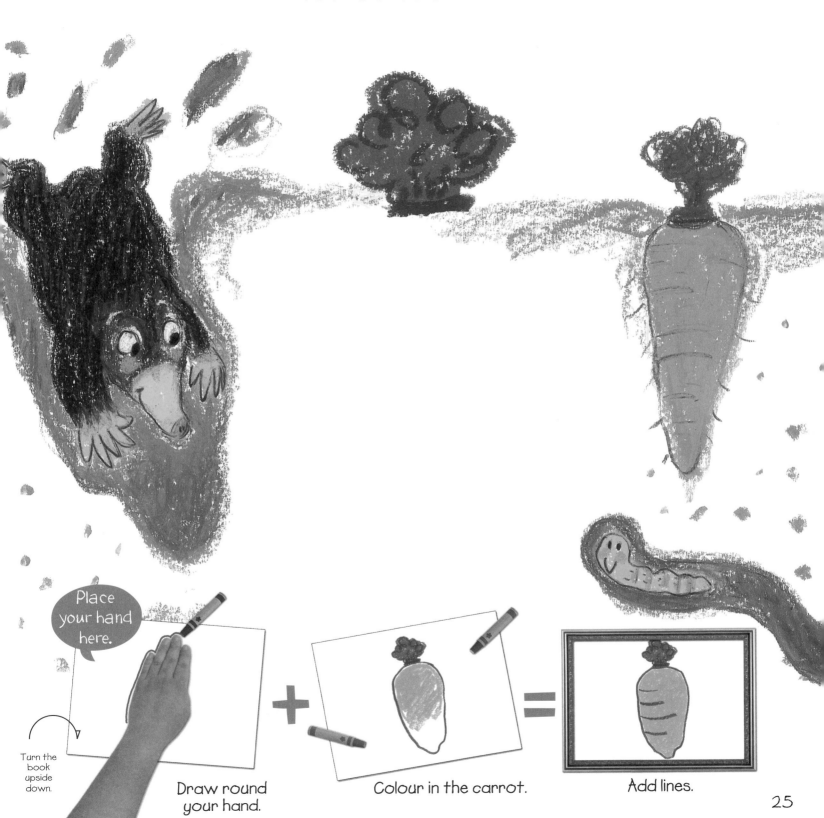

Place your hand here.

Turn the book upside down.

Draw round your hand.

Colour in the carrot.

Add lines.

25

Place your hand on the page to make a business man.

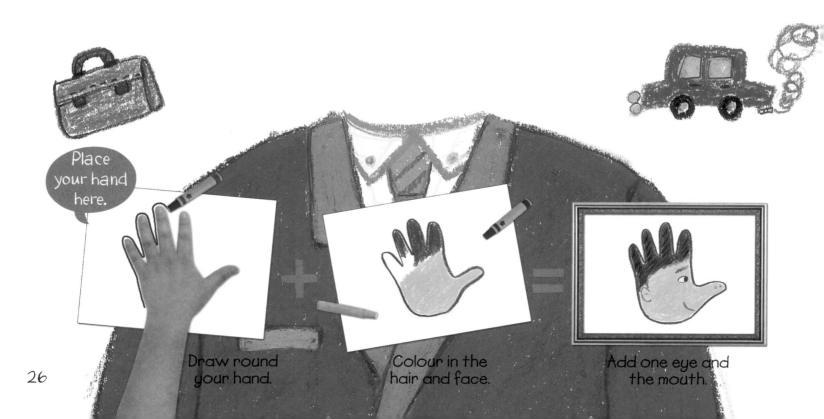

26

Place your hand here.

Draw round your hand.

Colour in the hair and face.

Add one eye and the mouth.

HAND ART

Place your hand on the page to make a professor.

Place your hand here.

Draw round your hand.

Colour in the hair and face.

Add a moustache, glasses and wrinkles.

Place your hand on the page to make a chef.

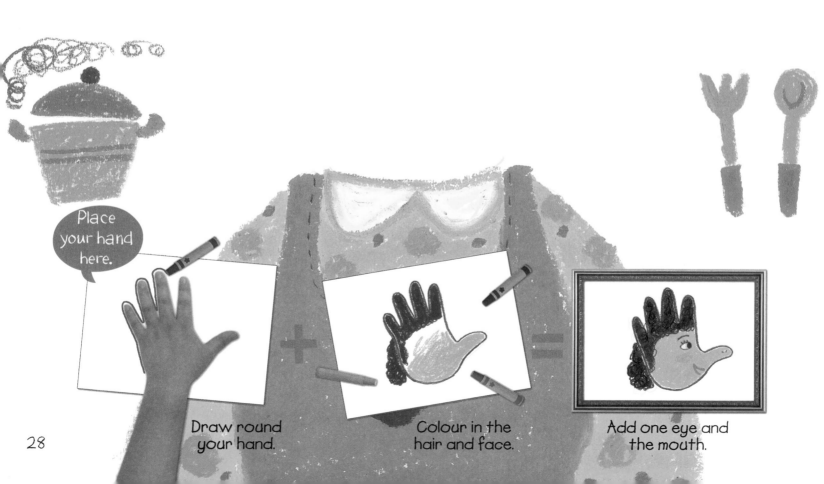

Place your hand here.

Draw round your hand.

Colour in the hair and face.

Add one eye and the mouth.

HAND ART

Place your hand on the page to make a **babysitter**.

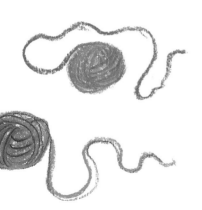

Place your hand here.

Draw round your hand.

Colour in the hair and face.

Add eyes, the mouth and a hairbun.

29

Place your hand on the page to make an **ear**.

Place your hand here.

Draw round your hand.

Colour in the ear.

Add lines.

30

Place your hand on the page to give the king a **crown**.

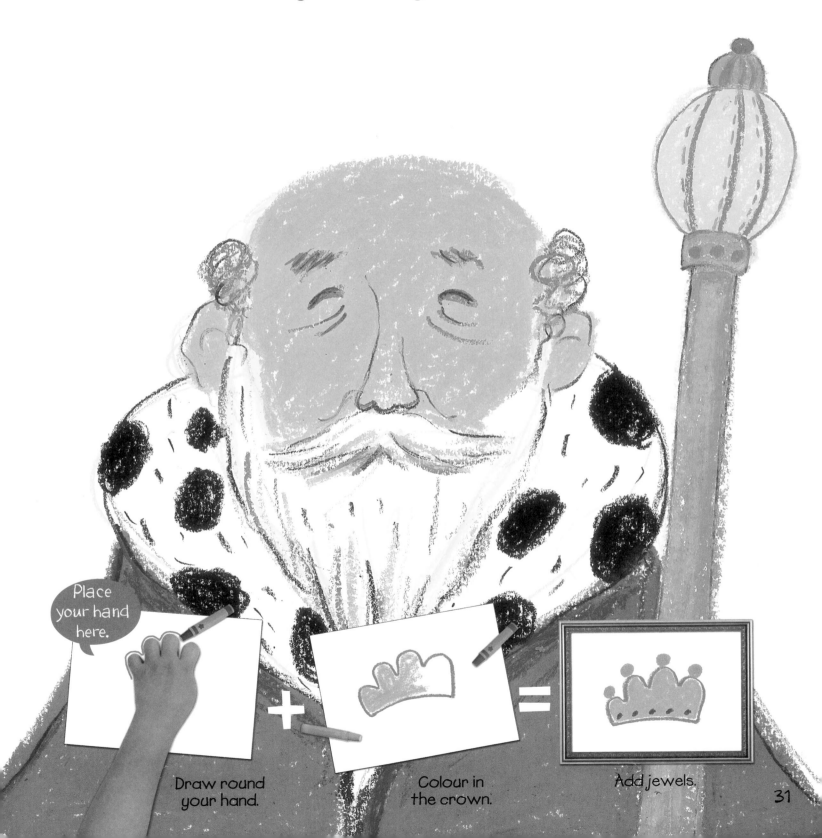

Place your hand here.

Draw round your hand.

+

Colour in the crown.

=

Add jewels.

31

Place your finger on the page to make a **prawn**.

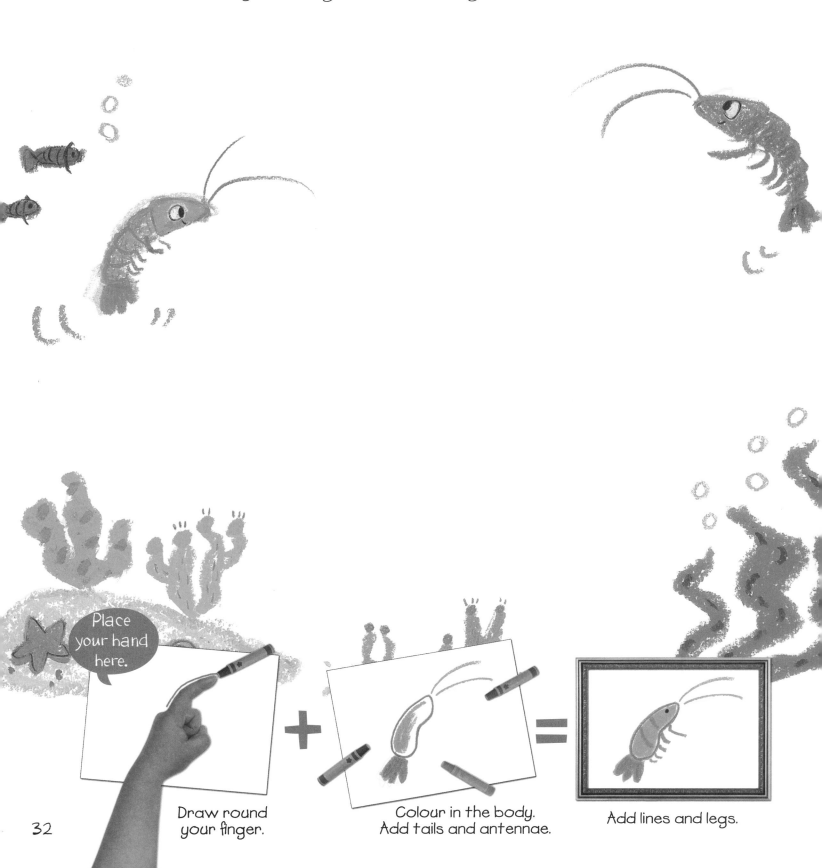

Place your hand here.

Draw round
your finger.

+

Colour in the body.
Add tails and antennae.

=

Add lines and legs.

 **HAND ART**

Place your hand on the page to make a crab.

Place your hand here.

Draw round your hand twice.

Colour in the legs, head and sharp claws.

Colour in the body.

33

 Place your hand on the page to make an **eagle**.

Place your hand here.

Draw round
34 your hand twice.

Colour in the wings.

Colour in the body.
Add feathers.

Place your hand on the page
to make a **peacock**.

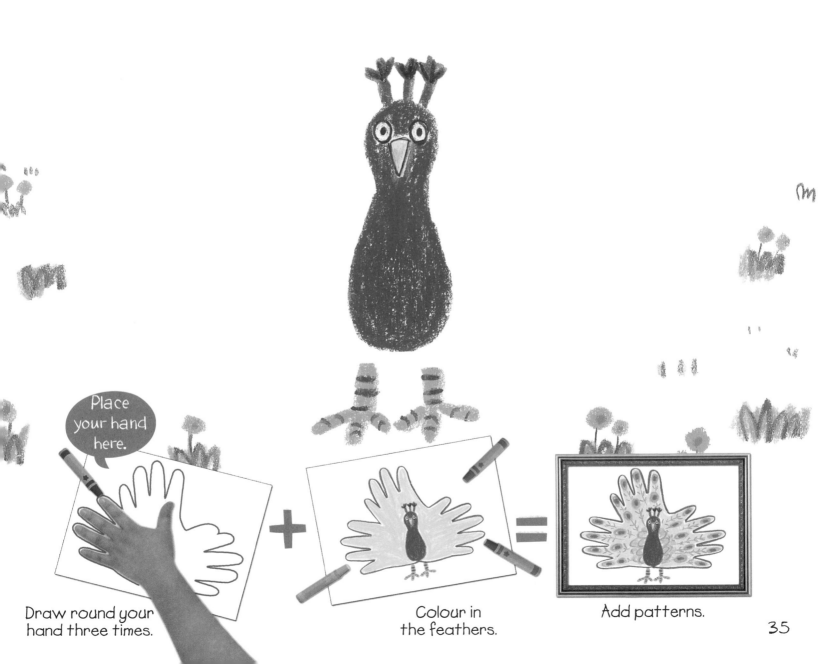

Place
your hand
here.

Draw round your
hand three times.

Colour in
the feathers.

Add patterns.

35

Place your hand on the page to
make footprints on the sand.

Place
your hand
here.

Make a handprint
using paint.

Start the toes with
coloured crayons.

Add all of the toes.

36

Place your hand on the page
to make a butterfly.

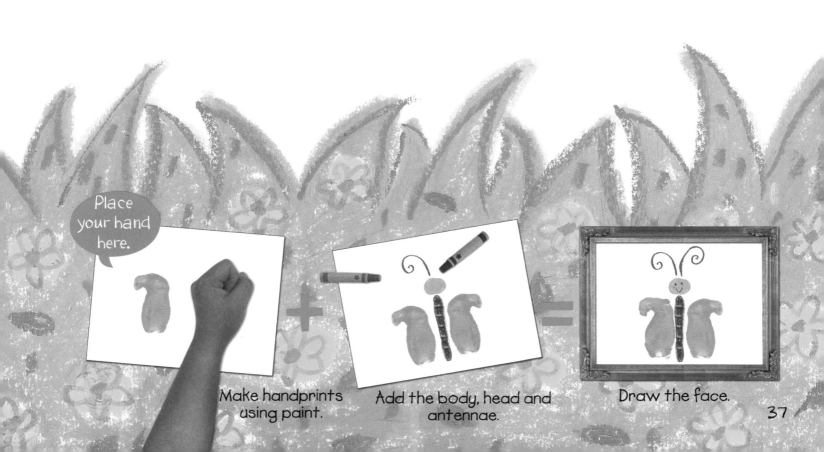

Place your hand here.

Make handprints using paint.

Add the body, head and antennae.

Draw the face.

37

Place your hand on the page to make a sun.

Place your hand here.

Make a handprint using paint.

Add more rays around the sun.

Add a face.

38

Place your hand on the page to make a galloping horse.

Place your hand here.

Turn the book upside down.

Make a handprint using paint.

Add the horse's mane.

Add hooves and a tail.

39

Place your hand on the page to finish the tiger.

Place your hand here.

Turn the book upside down.

Make a handprint using paint.

Draw in any bits of the head covered by paint.

Add stripes and claws.

Place your hand on the page to finish the elephant.

Place your hand here.

Turn the book upside down.

Make a handprint using paint.

+

Draw back in the eyes and trunk.

=

Add feet, a tail, the ear and stripes.

Place your finger on the page
to make a sunflower.

Place your finger here.

Dip your finger in some paint.

Make the petals.

Complete the flower.

 PRINT ART

Place your finger on the page to make a **swarm** of bees.

Place your finger here.

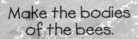
Make the bodies of the bees.

+

Add stripes, eyes, nose and antennae.

=

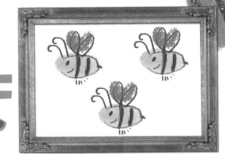
Add wings.

43

Place your finger on the page to make
the sparrows on the wire.

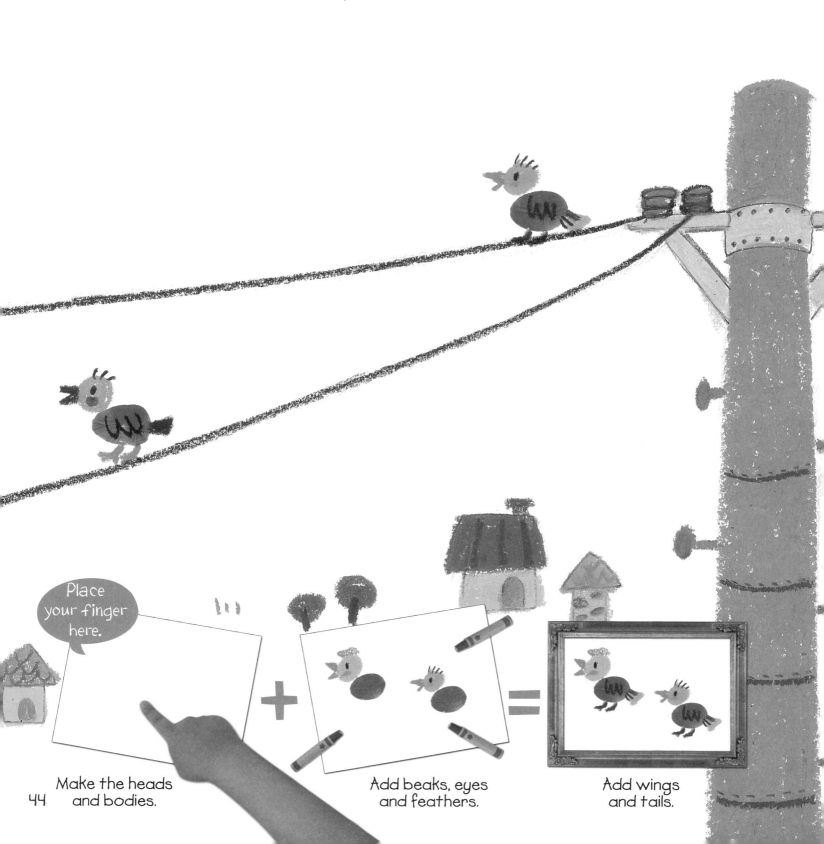

Place
your finger
here.

Make the heads
and bodies.

Add beaks, eyes
and feathers.

Add wings
and tails.

44

Place your finger on the page
to finish the lion's mane.

Place your finger here.

Dip your finger in
some paint.

+

Add the mane.

=

Complete the mane.

45

Place your finger on the page and add
the caterpillars to the cabbage.

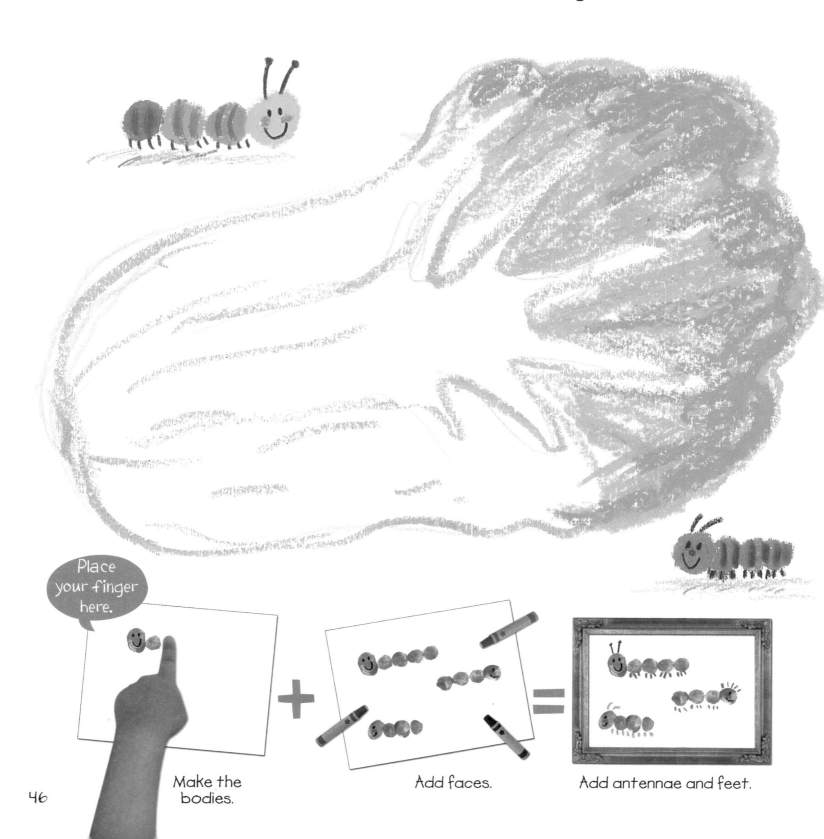

Place your finger here.

Make the bodies.

+

Add faces.

=

Add antennae and feet.

46

Place your finger on the page and add ants to the cookie.

Place your finger here.

Use your finger to make ant bodies.

Each body has three parts.

Add legs, a face and antennae.

47

 PALM PRINT

Turn this palm print into a submarine.

Add your own extras.

48

 PALM PRINT

Turn this palm print into a train.

Add your own extras.

49

 PALM PRINT

Turn this palm print into a happy face.

Add your own extras.

50

Turn this palm print into an angry face.

Add your own extras.

 PALM PRINT

Turn these palm prints into a ferris wheel.

Add your own extras.

Turn this palm print into a giraffe.

Add your own extras.

FINGERPRINT

Add your own extras.

Finish the bee, the butterfly and the flowers.

54

 FINGERPRINT Finish the markings on the dog and the cat.

Add your own extras.

55

Finish the scarecrow and birds.

Add your own extras.

56

Finish the go-karts.

Add your own extras.

Finish the bird.

Add your own extras.

Finish the lizard.

Add your own extras.

Create your own freestyle hand art.

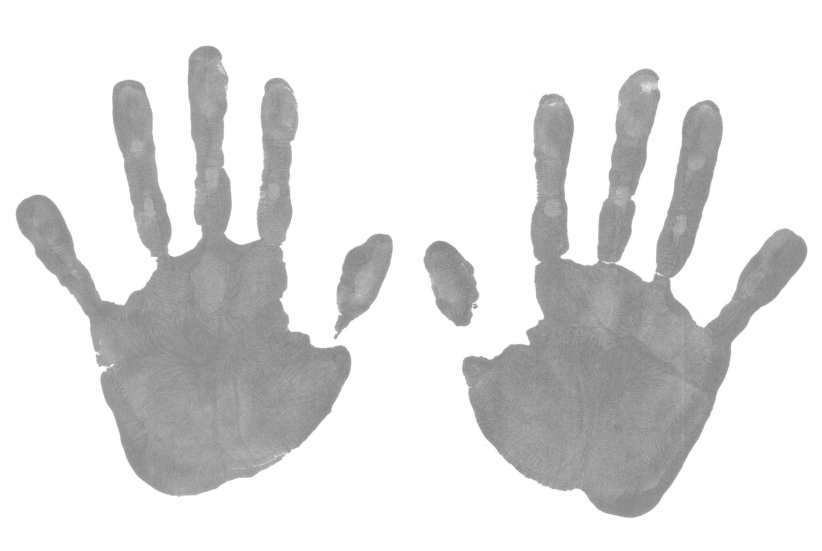

Create your own freestyle hand art.

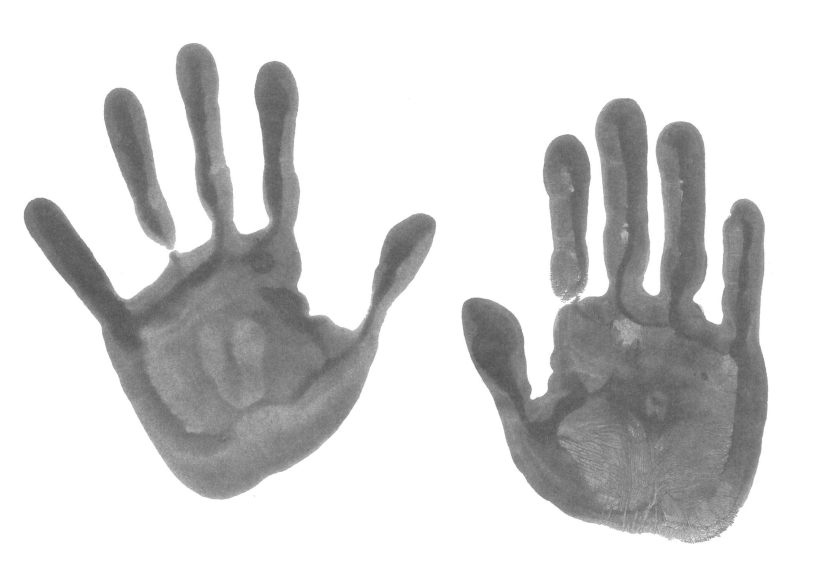

Create your own freestyle hand art.

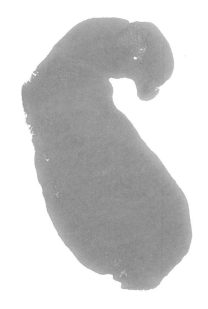

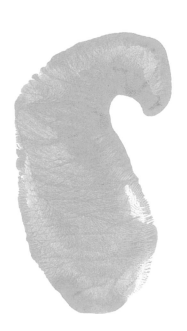

Create your own freestyle hand art.

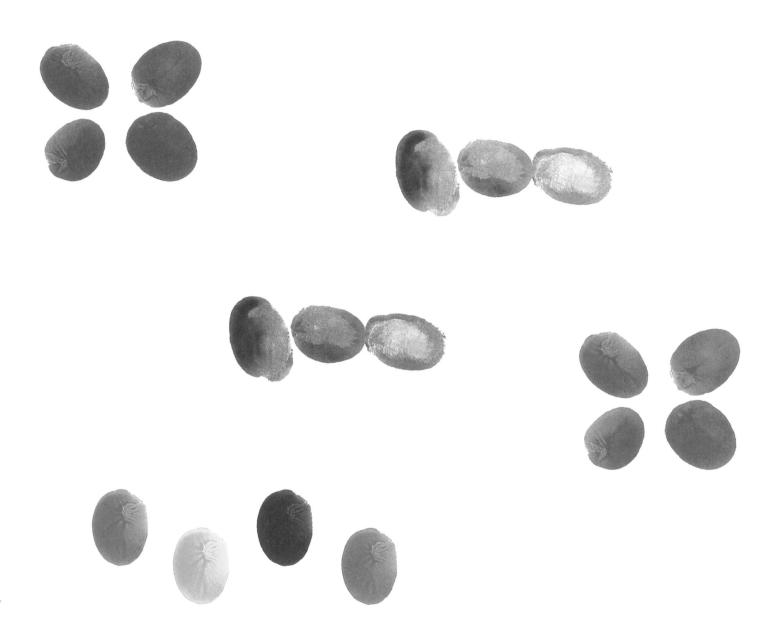

 FREESTYLE

Create your own freestyle hand art.